Dear Parent:

Congratulations! Your child is taking the first steps on an exciting journey. The destination? Independent reading!

STEP INTO READING® will help your child get there. The program offers five steps to reading success. Each step includes fun stories and colorful art. There are also Step into Reading Sticker Books, Step into Reading Math Readers, Step into Reading Phonics Readers, Step into Reading Write-In Readers, and Step into Reading Phonics Boxed Sets—a complete literacy program with something to interest every child.

Learning to Read, Step by Step!

Ready to Read   Preschool–Kindergarten
• big type and easy words • rhyme and rhythm • picture clues
For children who know the alphabet and are eager to begin reading.

Reading with Help   Preschool–Grade 1
• basic vocabulary • short sentences • simple stories
For children who recognize familiar words and sound out new words with help.

Reading on Your Own   Grades 1–3
• engaging characters • easy-to-follow plots • popular topics
For children who are ready to read on their own.

Reading Paragraphs   Grades 2–3
• challenging vocabulary • short paragraphs • exciting stories
For newly independent readers who read simple sentences with confidence.

Ready for Chapters   Grades 2–4
• chapters • longer paragraphs • full-color art
For children who want to take the plunge into chapter books but still like colorful pictures.

STEP INTO READING® is designed to give every child a successful reading experience. The grade levels are only guides. Children can progress through the steps at their own speed, developing confidence in their reading, no matter what their grade.

Remember, a lifetime love of reading starts with a single step!

For Luther and his friend Cole—
two boys I am lucky to know —C.M.H.

To my friend Jane and her
love for kale —B.S.

Text copyright © 2013 by Charise Mericle Harper
Cover and interior illustrations copyright © 2013 by Bob Shea

All rights reserved. Published in the United States by Random House Children's Books, a division of Random House, Inc., New York.

Step into Reading, Random House, and the Random House colophon are registered trademarks of Random House, Inc.

Visit us on the Web!
StepIntoReading.com
randomhouse.com/kids
Educators and librarians, for a variety of teaching tools, visit us at
RHTeachersLibrarians.com

Library of Congress Cataloging-in-Publication Data
Harper, Charise Mericle.
  Wedgieman to the rescue / by Charise Harper ; illustrated by Bob Shea.
    p. cm. – (The adventures of Wedgieman ; #2)
  Summary: Superhero Veggieman, better known as Wedgieman, faces off against Bad Dude, an inventor whose Make-Things-Disappear Machine causes trouble on the playground.
  ISBN 978-0-307-93072-9 (pbk.) – ISBN 978-0-375-97059-7 (gibraltar library binding)
  [1. Superheroes–Fiction. 2. Inventors–Fiction. 3. Vegetables–Fiction. 4. Humorous stories.]
  I. Shea, Bob, ill. II. Title.
  PZ7.H231323Wet 2013
  [E]–dc23 2011047692

Printed in the United States of America   10 9 8 7 6 5 4 3 2 1

WEDGIEMAN
TO THE RESCUE

SALAD BAR

The ADVENTURES of
WEDGIEMAN

By Charise Mericle Harper

Illustrated by Bob Shea

Random House New York

There was a new superhero in town.

His name was Veggieman,

but he had another name, too—

Wedgieman.

His new name was a mistake.

But it was the children's favorite!

"Yay! Wedgieman!" they cheered.

Wedgieman was strong,

he could fly,

he had X-ray eyes,

and he really liked vegetables.

"I will fight crime and make sure children eat their vegetables!" said Wedgieman.

Crunch! He bit some celery.

Wedgieman was happy.

There was a bad guy.

He lived on the other side of town.

The bad guy's name was Larry.

"I need a better name," said Larry.

He thought, and thought, and thought.

Finally, he said, "I know!

I'll call myself Bad Dude!"

Bad Dude made himself a

bad dude outfit.

"Perfect!" said Bad Dude.

His brain was filled with bad ideas.

Bad Dude was happy.

Bad Dude had a secret hideout.

It was filled with inventions.

The inventions were incredible
and amazing,
but Bad Dude had made them,
so they were also dangerous . . .
and bad.
It was safe to say that Bad
Dude was the baddest
dude in town.

Bad Dude went to the bottom of a hill.

He had one of his inventions with him.

It was a big, heavy machine.

It is not easy to get

a big, heavy thing up a hill.

Bad Dude did a lot of sweating.

Finally, he made it.

"I love this Make-Things-Disappear
Machine," said Bad Dude,
and he gave the machine a pat.
Bad Dude had a plan.
It was a bad plan.
A bad plan with two parts.

Part one: Zap everything
on the playground.

Part two: Make all the children work
in the Bad Dude factory!

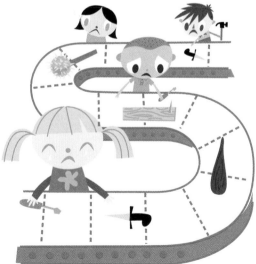

Bad Dude smiled
and pointed his machine
at the playground slide.
"Part one!" he shouted,
and pushed a button.
ZAP!

The slide disappeared,
and a small girl fell on her bottom.

"Perfect!" said
Bad Dude,
and he laughed
an evil laugh.

At first the girl was surprised.
Then she was sad.
"Waaaaahhh!" cried the girl.

Back on the other side of town,
Wedgieman heard the girl.
"Oh no! Someone is in trouble!"
said Wedgieman.

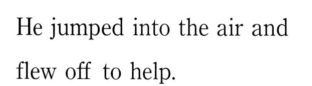

He jumped into the air and
flew off to help.

Wedgieman landed on the playground.

THUMP!

The children pointed to a hill.

"Up there!" they cried.

Wedgieman ran up the hill.

He saw Bad Dude and his big machine.

"Who are you? Stop at once!"
said Wedgieman.

"Never!" said Bad Dude.

"I'm Bad Dude,
and you can't stop me!"

Bad Dude gave Wedgieman an evil grin.

He pointed his machine and said,

"Now I will make you disappear!"

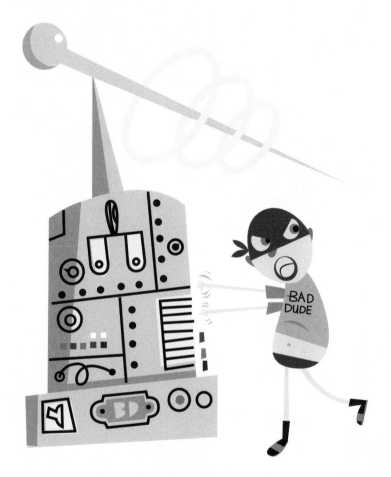

ZAP!

Wedgieman jumped into the air.

A small tree behind him
suddenly disappeared.

"Yikes!" said Wedgieman.

"You *are* a bad dude!

 Stop at once!"

"Try and make me!" said Bad Dude.

"Okay!" said Wedgieman.

There was a fight.

"Give him a wedgie!" yelled a boy.

"Make it a big one!" yelled a girl.

And then the fight was over.

Wedgieman was the winner.

The big, heavy machine was broken.

Bad Dude was trapped on the ground.

A small boy pointed to Bad Dude.

The boy started to laugh.

"*D-u-d-e* spells *doodie*," said the boy.

"No it doesn't!" said Bad Dude.

Bad Dude was angry.

"Boo, Bad Doodie! Doodie! Doodie!"
shouted the children.

Now Bad Dude was *really* angry.

Wedgieman shook his head.

He looked at the happy children.

"Don't be angry," said Wedgieman.

"These children can't help it.

They can't spell."

Bad Dude didn't care about spelling.

He was still mad.

THE END—OR IS IT?

It was time to take Bad Dude to jail.
"Evil never wins," said Wedgieman.
He picked up Bad Dude and
slung him over his shoulder.
"Give him a wedgie!"
shouted the children.

Wedgieman looked at Bad Dude.

Bad Dude looked worried.

Wedgieman had a different idea.

"Wedgie after veggie," said Wedgieman.

He passed out a healthy snack.

There was enough celery for everyone.

The children ate quickly.

After the last bite, they shouted,

"Wedgie time! Wedgie time! Wedgie time!"

They jumped up and
down with excitement.

"Okay," said Wedgieman.

Bad Dude shook his head.

"Don't worry, Bad Dude,"

said Wedgieman.

"The wedgies are only for me."

Wedgieman put Bad Dude
down next to a tree.

He turned around
and looked over his
shoulder.

"This one's the Celery!"
he called back.
And then he did it!

It was an awesome wedgie.

"Yay! Wedgieman!"

cheered the children.

"Wedgieman is our hero!"

shouted a girl.

Wedgieman picked up Bad Dude and

walked toward the jail.

Everyone was happy,

even Bad Dude.